HOW TO BE COOLER THAN COOL

For Ada, one cool chick
ST

For Lou and Hugo, the coolest Wolf and Bear around
JJ

CANDLEWICK PRESS

Text copyright © 2021 by Sean Taylor. Illustrations copyright © 2021 by Jean Jullien. All rights reserved. No part of this book may be reproduced, transmitted, or stored in an information retrieval system in any form or by any means, graphic, electronic, or mechanical, including photocopying, taping, and recording, without prior written permission from the publisher. First US edition 2021. Library of Congress Catalog Card Number pending. ISBN 978-1-5362-1529-8. This book was typeset in URW Egyptienne T and Futura Bold. The illustrations were done in ink and colored digitally. Candlewick Press, 99 Dover Street, Somerville, Massachusetts 02144. www.candlewick.com.
Printed in Humen, Dongguan, China. 21 22 23 24 25 26 APS 10 9 8 7 6 5 4 3 2 1

Sean Taylor   Jean Jullien

HOW TO BE COOLER THAN COOL

Look what Cat found.

These sunglasses.

"You know what," she said.

"I'm not just any old cat at the playground.

I'm a real cool cat who can glide backward down

the slide, looking cooler than cool . . .

WITH EXTRA COOL ON TOP!"

But . . .

UH-OH!

Now look what Cockatoo found . . .

"You know what," he said.
"I'm not just any old cockatoo.
I'm a supercool cockatoo
who can dance coolly along the seesaw,
doing the supercool cockatoo boogaloo!"

And guess what Pig found . . .

"You know what," he said.
"I'm not just any old pig.
I'm a totally cool pig who can
stand up on the swing looking
so completely cooler than cool
that everyone's going to call me
Mr. Totally Completely Cool!"

Pig smiled.

"EVEN
MY
PANTS
ARE
COOL."

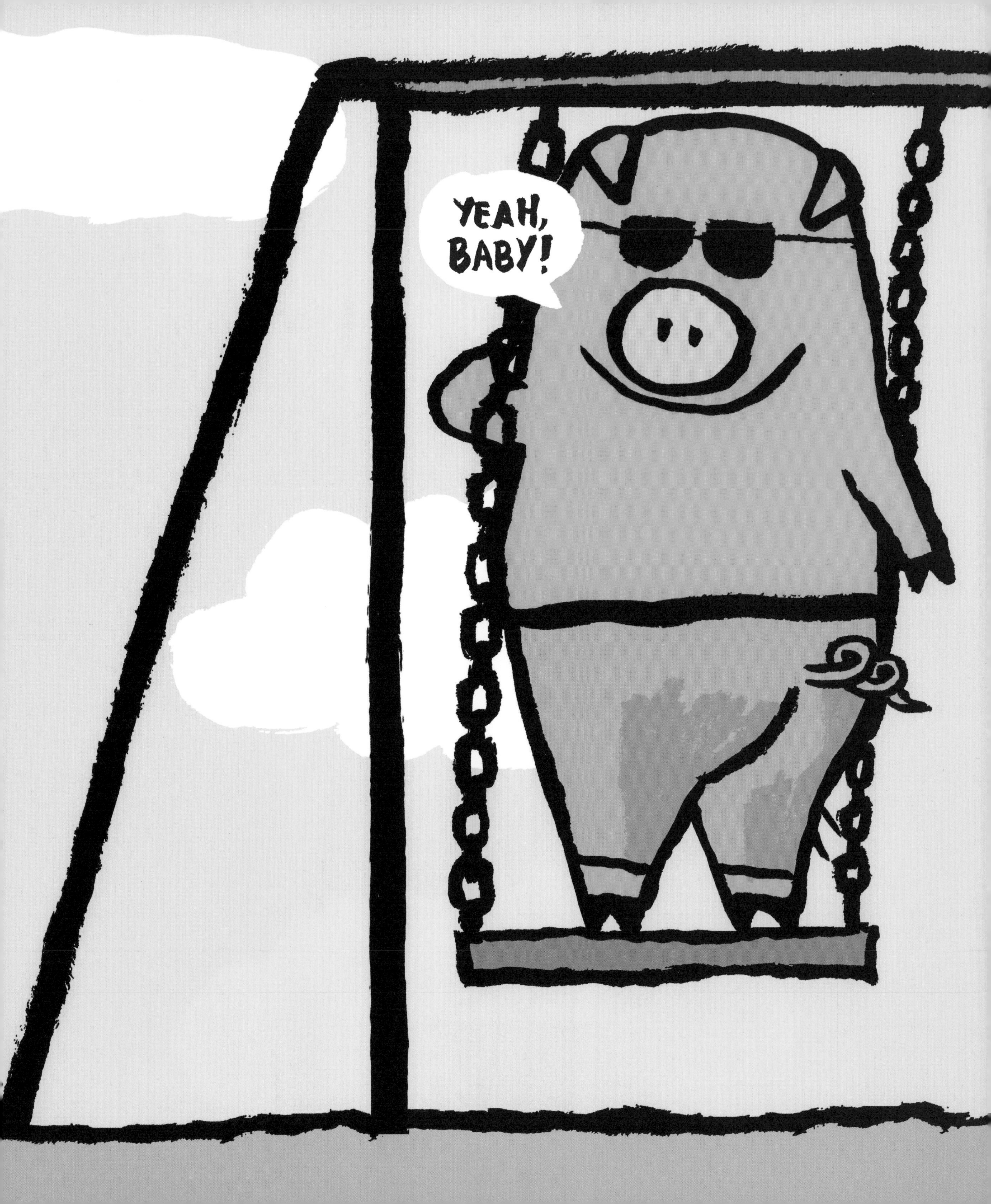
YEAH, BABY!

But . . .

UH-OH!

OH, NO!

WHOA!

Pig said, "I don't think I managed to look cooler than cool just then."

Cat and Cockatoo shook their heads. "You didn't."

Then Cat said,
"You don't look cool when
you've got sunglasses
on your bottom."

They were all disappointed.

The sunglasses hadn't made them cool, after all.

Then Chick came along.

"Oh, YEAH!" she said. "Look what I've found!"

"Watch out!" Cockatoo told her.

Cat added, "They'll make you try to
glide coolly down the slide
or dance coolly along the seesaw
or stand up coolly on the swing."

"BUT IT WON'T BE COOL!" said Pig.

Chick still put them on.

She said, "I'm just going to
slide down the slide,
seesaw on the seesaw,
and swing on the swing.

Come on!"

EASY.

They did. Nobody tried to be cool.

Soon they were sliding,
seesawing, and swinging together.

And you know what?